James Otis

Under the Liberty Tree

James Otis

Under the Liberty Tree

ISBN/EAN: 9783337336950

Printed in Europe, USA, Canada, Australia, Japan

Cover: Foto ©Andreas Hilbeck / pixelio.de

More available books at **www.hansebooks.com**

UNDER THE LIBERTY TREE

A STORY OF

THE "BOSTON MASSACRE"

BY

JAMES OTIS

AUTHOR OF "JENNY WREN'S BOARDING-HOUSE," "JERRY'S FAMILY"
"THE BOYS' REVOLT," "THE BOYS OF 1745," ETC.

Illustrated

BOSTON
ESTES AND LAURIAT
1896

CONTENTS.

LIST OF ILLUSTRATIONS.

"YOUR LORDSHIP must know that Liberty Tree is a large, old Elm in the High Street, upon which the effigies were hung in the time of the Stamp Act, and from whence the mobs at that time made their parades. It has since been adorned with an inscription, and has obtained the name of Liberty Tree, as the ground under it has that of Liberty Hall. In August last, just before the commencement of the present troubles, they erected a flagstaff, which went through the tree, and a good deal above the top of the tree. Upon this they hoist a flag as a signal for the Sons of Liberty, as they are called."

Extract from a letter written by Governor Bernard to Lord Hillsborough under date of June 18, 1768.

"The world should never forget the spot where once stood Liberty Tree, so famous in your annals."

The Marquis de Lafayette, in a speech delivered in Boston during his last visit to America.

UNDER THE LIBERTY TREE

A Story of the "Boston Massacre"

CHAPTER I.

THE LIBERTY TREE.

IT was on the evening of February 21, 1770, in the city
of Boston, that a party of boys, ranging in age from ten
to eighteen years, were assembled at what was known as
"Liberty Hall," which was not a building, but simply the
open space sheltered by the wide-spreading branches of
the "Liberty Tree."

Although General Gage's troops occupied the city, and
patrols of the "bloody backs," as the red-coated soldiers
had been called in derision, paced to and fro at regular
intervals along the streets, these boys spoke openly of
their desire, and even of their intention, to avenge the
wrongs under which the colonists were suffering, believing
from past experience that the troops would not dare pro-
ceed to extremities with the citizens, more especially since

Lieutenant-Governor Hutchinson "doubted his authority to order the soldiers to fire upon the populace." *

These boys had shown several times in the vicinity of this same so-called Liberty Hall of what acts they were capable, and there was not one of them but that looked forward to the time when it should be possible to do something more than simply vent his displeasure in words.

They had been among the throng who, in open defiance of the law, had made prisoner of Giles Hendricks; tarred and feathered, and then carried him in a cart through the principal streets of the city to the Liberty Tree, because he had given evidence regarding the smuggling of wine from Rhode Island. Here under the old elm he had been forced to swear he would never be guilty of a like crime in the future, and only then was allowed to go free, wearing his closely fitting and decidedly uncomfortable garment of tar.

The gathering on this particular night at Liberty Hall was, in the opinion of those participating, of great importance.

Several shopkeepers had failed to keep the promise not to import British goods, made in January, and on the afternoon of this day, Hardy Baker, who was apprenticed to Master Piemont, the barber, had learned that Theophilus Lillie, whose shop was on Hanover Street, near the New Brick Church, had not only broken his agreement, but openly declared it was his intention to sell whatsoever he pleased.

"He boasts he will sell even tea, if it so be his customers wish to buy," Master Baker said, in concluding his story of the shopkeeper's iniquities.

"How did you learn this?" Amos Richardson asked, quite sharply, for the barber's apprentice was noted rather for his imaginative powers than a strict adherence to the truth.

"I heard it when I went to the Custom House this morning."

"But what were you doing there? How long is it since you have been hobnobbing in that quarter?"

"Am I accused of being friendly with the 'bloody backs'?" Hardy asked, indignantly. "Can't I go anywhere in the town but that suspicions are aroused?"

"It will be well for you to show anger only after you have explained why you were at the Custom House."

"There is no reason why I should be forced to do so. The part I took in bringing Hendricks to the Liberty Tree is enough to show that the 'bloody backs' can expect no favour from me."

"Yet your master has among his customers many who wear coats of red, and you shave some of them."

"True; but it is not every one over whose face my razor passes, that I call a friend. Since you are so suspicious, Amos Richardson, I will explain my going to the Custom House," Hardy added, only after noting the fact that several of those standing nearest were gazing at him sternly. "You must know that many of the Britishers who come to Master Piemont's shop to be served pay for the work at the end of every three months, instead of doing so each day or week. Now, among these redcoats who hold on to their money as long as possible, is one Lieutenant Draper, whom I attend. When it was learned that he intended to let his account run until three months had passed, Master Piemont told me the bill should be mine in consideration of my strict attention to duty. Master Piemont knows a good workman when he sees one, and I have been in his shop a long while."

"But you are not a workman yet," a member of the party shouted. "You are only an apprentice, Hardy."

"Well, and if I am? I may be as good as a journeyman for all that. If I was n't, it is hardly lik 'v Master

Piemont would have made me so generous an offer, and of his own free will."

"Perhaps he thought it was the only way by which he could induce you to attend to your work," some one shouted, laughingly, and Amos said, sharply:

"We have not come here to make sport. Let him explain, without interruption, why he was at the Custom House this morning, and then we will decide how we can best bring Master Lillie to realise that he must keep the agreement made with the other shopkeepers. What has Lieutenant Draper and his account to do with your visit, Hardy?"

"It has everything to do, since I was there attending to my own business. The officer's quarterly bill should have been paid last Thursday, and, knowing he was on duty at the place, I went there in the hope of getting my money. Does that seem reasonable?"

Amos looked around inquiringly at his companions, and Chris Snyder, a German lad only eleven years of age, but who was allowed a voice in the meetings beneath the Liberty Tree because of his staunch loyalty and unfailing good nature, cried, impatiently:

"Let him tell his story. I am certain he has spoken nothing but the truth, for he said to me last night that he had twice asked for the money, and was going this morning for the third time."

"Did you get it, Hardy?" some one asked, and Master Baker replied, angrily:

"I did not; but the next time I demand it he will pay,

for I shall treat him with no more ceremony than I would one of the pirates."

"Be careful you don't feel the flat of his sword across your back, my old barber."

"He dares not strike me, for he knows how much influence I have in this town."

"And how much have you? When did you become of great public importance?"

"When I showed what should be done to reformers like Hendricks."

"And are you the one who is responsible for that lesson?"

"But for me it might never have been given, for I pointed out the man when it was not believed he was in the city."

"We are wasting our time," Amos cried, impatiently, raising his voice above the uproar, for now many had begun to deride Hardy's pretensions. "Let him explain how he knows that Master Theophilus Lillie has declared he will sell British goods."

The barber's apprentice was prompt to make reply, for the taunts of his comrades were not at all to his liking.

"While waiting in the guard-room at the Custom House, I heard the 'bloody backs' talking among themselves about the spirit which Theophilus was showing in declaring he would conduct his business to please himself. There was among the soldiers one who had heard him announce his decision to no less a person than Master Samuel Adams; but in order to make more certain of the truth, I went to the shop as if I had been sent by Master Piemont, and asked for tea. It was Theophilus Lillie himself who told me he had it. Do you want stronger proof than that?"

Although Hardy Baker was not noted for strict loyalty to the truth, there was no one among the party who doubted his statement, and immediately the question arose as to what should be done to bring the offending shop-keeper to a full realisation of the enormity of his offence.

While the bolder spirits were discussing among themselves as to whether the general public would look with favour upon their treating the merchant as they had the informer, and the more timid ones were arguing that their elders might not countenance an act of violence against a merchant occupying such a prominent position in the mercantile world as did Master Theophilus Lillie, James Gray, a lad small of stature but fertile in expedients, as had been shown many times under similar circumstances, made a suggestion which met with the unqualified approval of all.

"I have at home the figurehead of the old sloop *Faith and Prudence*. It is the image of a man, with a nose not unlike the one Master Lillie carries on his face. Let us saw the head off, nail it to a pole, and set it up in front of his shop with a notice attached warning all honest citizens against trading with him."

"Hurrah for Jim Gray's plan!" a member of the party cried, and heartily the others responded, causing one of two old gentlemen, who chanced to be passing at that moment, to say, with many an ominous shake of his white head :

"If the children are allowed to display signs of disloyalty thus publicly, it is not difficult to say how treasonable must be their parents.   Governor Hutchinson shows far too mild a spirit, or some of these young sparks would be adorning the pillory.   It was not so when I was a boy."

"But it may be they are bent only on some youthful frolic, Friend Johnson, and we gray - heads must make allowance for young blood."

"The only allowance they should have is a dozen strokes of the whip.   They are indulging in treasonable practices, otherwise the meeting-place would not be under what is already known throughout the colony as the Liberty Tree.   I shall speak with Governor Hutchinson to-morrow, and if he still insists upon faint - hearted measures, word must be sent to his majesty.   Unless this lawless spirit is speedily checked, trouble will follow. The fathers of these young scoundrels may prudently contrive to keep themselves from publicly committing any overt act against the laws ; but they can be taught a lesson through their sons."

Before the old gentlemen were beyond sight of the Tree, the meeting had noisily adjourned to Jim Gray's home on Cross Street, the entire party marching with something approaching military precision through the streets, as if fancying this semblance of order was necessary to give proper dignity to what they knew would be a riotous act.

The figurehead of the sloop had been long exposed to the weather in the rear of the house, and perhaps no one save Jim and his assistants could have traced a resemblance in the roughly-hewn contour of the face to that of the prosperous merchant. They, however, were well satisfied with the instrument which might bring Master Lillie to a realisation of his offence, and Hardy Baker was positive no citizen of Boston could look upon the wooden face without seeing in it a strong resemblance to the trader who had broken his agreement.

The head was severed from the trunk and affixed to the mast of Amos Richardson's sailboat, which spar was willingly sacrificed for that purpose by its owner.

The majority of the party appeared to think that the head in itself would serve as a menace to Master Lillie; but Jim Gray was not satisfied with so mild a warning, and proceeded, after his own fashion, to add to its supposed terrors.

He found in the wood-house a piece of planed board, three feet long and fifteen or sixteen inches in width, on which he inscribed, after much labour, with paint composed of lampblack and fish-oil, the name of each of the merchants who had been guilty of breaking their agreement regarding the sale of British goods.

This he nailed on the spar within a few feet of the head, affixing it so firmly that it could not readily be wrenched off, and the instrument of warning was held erect a few moments that the young conspirators might observe the general effect.

"Master Lillie will quake in his boots when he sees that," Hardy Baker said, in a tone of conviction. "Nothing could be better, unless we had his name with the others."

"But the head is there," Jim replied, "and even Master Lillie himself must see that the face is like to his."

"Unless he is over-fond of looking in a mirror, he may make a mistake," Hardy persisted. "Can't you put his name on the board with the others?"

Jim was not disposed to add to what he considered almost a work of art, lest he should detract from its merits in some degree, and after a brief pause he said, as a happy thought occurred to him :

"This will look better, and there can be no mistake if the spar is put up with the board set in the proper direction."

As he spoke he painted a rude hand with the dexter finger pointing.

"Now we have only to place it so that this shows the way into the shop, and if Master Lillie makes any mistake in regard to its being intended for him, he has a thicker skull than his neighbors credit him with."

It appeared to the party assembled as if nothing was wanting to make this symbol of warning full of meaning and menace, and it only remained to place it in position.

Hardy Baker proposed to set out at once to complete the work, regardless of the fact that the citizens were yet astir, and that the moon illumined the streets almost brilliantly, thereby preventing secrecy of movement.

Amos Richardson insisted that it might be fatal to the success of the scheme if they were discovered by Master Lillie before the pole had been set in place, and suggested that a certain number be selected to perform the work at an hour when all good people were supposed to be asleep.

The only difficulty in acting upon this suggestion was that every member of the party was desirous of doing a portion of the work; but Amos held firm to the idea that they might defeat their purpose by allowing too large a body of workmen to take part, and that the smallest number needed to perform the task would have greater chance of success.

Therefore it was that Jim, who was entitled to a place on the " committee " because of having designed the symbol ; Amos, owing to the fact that he was looked upon by his comrades as their leader ; Hardy Baker, because he had a personal grievance against the British and, consequently, against British goods, through his unsatisfied claim against the lieutenant, and little Chris Snyder were finally selected as the boys to perform the more delicate portion of the task.

Very reluctantly the others took their departure, leaving the four to complete the work after their own fashion, and promising to be in front of Master Lillie's shop at an early hour next morning.

Being thus left to their own devices, the " committee " took refuge in the wood-shed, for the night seemed uncomfortably cold, save when a fellow was indulging in plenty of exercise, and there they remained, looking out of the open door at the result of Jim's handiwork ten minutes or more without speaking, when Chris Snyder broke the silence by asking, in his thin, piping voice :

"What are you fellows waiting here for ?   Why don't we carry the thing up to Master Lillie's shop at once ?   It won't be a hard job for four of us, and I must be getting home.   Mother says a boy of my age ought not to be out-of-doors after nine o'clock."

"And that's where your mother is right, Chris," Amos replied, with a laugh.   "We shall all get the reputation of being very dissolute lads if the meetings at the Liberty Tree are continued many weeks longer.   As a matter of fact, I think you had best go home now."

"Why ?   I am one who was chosen to help place this warning in front of Master Lillie's shop."

"You wasn't selected with the idea that you would be of very much assistance, Chris.   I think the other fellows wanted to confer an honour upon you, even though you are the youngest of the party.   That's what comes of always being good-natured, and ready to do a comrade a friendly turn.   We shall get this pole into position without your help, and you might find yourself in trouble at home by remaining out-of-doors as long as I think it will be necessary for us to stay."

"Aren't you going to work at once ?"

"I don't think it will be safe until one o'clock," Amos replied, decidedly, and Hardy Baker exclaimed, petulantly :

"That's foolishness !   It is after ten now, and we

sha' n't see a dozen people between here and Hanover Street. Are you afraid, Amos?"

" Do you think it ? "

" I asked the question, that's all."

" If I thought you really meant it I should have a little task to perform now, before we set about Master Lillie's business, in giving you a warning against letting your tongue run away with your wits."

" I was only in sport, Amos," Hardy hastened to say, as he understood that his friend was angry. " Of course I did n't suppose for a moment you were afraid ; but it seems to me as if we might get through with the work at once, rather than wait around here all night. The ʻbloody backs' won't dare touch us so long as we are simply walk- ing through the streets, even though we *are* carrying a pole."

Jim Gray appeared to be of the same opinion, and Amos, understanding that his companions did not recog - nise the necessity for so much prudence, gave way.

" If we wait till past midnight there will be no mistake about doing as we wish, while to set out now may bring us into trouble," he said, thoughtfully. " However, if you are of the mind that we should go on with the work at this hour, taking all the chances of failure, I am ready."

" Come on, then ! " Jim shouted, as he seized one end of the pole. " I want to do my share of the work, and at the same time, slip into bed before daylight."

" How are we to fasten it when we get there?" Chris asked.

"The best way will be to dig a hole, and set it down so far that it cannot be pulled over without considerable labor," Hardy suggested, and Jim added :

"There's a spade in the woodhouse.   Let Chris bring that along, and the rest of us will carry the pole."

"Something more than that will be necessary, because the ground is frozen.   Look around for an axe ; we shall be obliged to work our way through the frost," Amos cried.

Chris found the necessary implements without difficulty, and, desirous of having the spar affixed so firmly there could be no question of overturning it readily, Hardy thrust into his pocket a piece of stout Manilla rope.

Thus equipped, the party set out.

Contrary to Amos's anticipations, they met no person during the walk from Cross Street to Hanover, near the New Brick Church, where was situated Master Theophilus Lillie's shop.

This quarter of the city appeared to be deserted, and the boys, working noiselessly but rapidly, soon had such an excavation, despite the frozen ground, as permitted of setting the spar at least two feet below the surface, and within a couple of yards of the shopkeeper's door.   Then, by packing the clods of frosty earth around it, the symbol of warning was soon as firm as could have been desired.

"Now help me to climb up there," Hardy whispered to Amos, as he took the rope from his pocket and pointed to the top of the spar.

"What are you going to do?"

"Tie the pole to a limb of that tree, and then Master Lillie may dig around the bottom as much as he pleases, for he will not be able to dislodge it unless he does as I am about to do."

Amos realised the wisdom of Hardy's plan, and, giving him the required "leg up," the warning was speedily attached to a limb of the tree in such a manner that considerable labour would be necessary in order to overthrow it.

Then the boys walked to the opposite side of the street and surveyed the result of their toil, after which Amos said, in a whisper:

"Now then, lads, we must get under cover. I don't fancy Master Lillie would attempt to make any serious trouble, even if he knew who put the ornament into position; but it is just as well that he and every one else is kept in ignorance of our share in the work. I shall be here as soon after daylight as possible, and reckon by that time there will be a bigger crowd around the shop than has been seen for many a day."

Then the conspirators separated, each going to his own home, and there was not in the minds of a single member of the party the slightest forebodings of the terrible tragedy which was to follow their attempt to teach Master Theophilus Lillie his duty.

CHAPTER II.

ON the morning following the assembly at Liberty Hall, which resulted in the warning given to Master Theophilus Lillie, Hardy Baker, regardless of the fact that Lieutenant Draper's account had been given him in consideration of strict attention to duty, went from his home directly to Hanover Street, instead of to the hair-dressing establishment of Master Piemont, as he should have done.

Once on Hanover Street, all thought of duty was forgotten as he viewed, with no slight degree of pride, that scene of excitement, in the cause of which he had assisted.

The pole, surmounted by the mutilated figurehead of the sloop and decorated with the names of the merchants who had been faithless to their agreement, was yet in position, as he and his companions had left it a short time previous, and, although the new day was but half an hour old, the throng in front of Master Lillie's shop was so great as to entirely block the street.

The first passerby, after the darkness of night was so far dissipated that the object could be readily distinguished, had stopped several moments to read the inscription — a difficult task, owing to the faint light. While deciphering, with no slight amount of labour, the result of Jim Gray's work as a painter, the man had been joined by one and another, until the walk directly in front of the shop was crowded to overflowing with the curious, the throng swelling far out into the street, and added to each moment, until, when Hardy Baker arrived, it had become a mob — a good-natured, careless gathering, but yet a mob, which needed but slight provocation to render it unmanageable and dangerous.

It filled Hardy Baker's sensation-loving heart with joy to see the result of the labour in which he had assisted.

For the moment he forgot that the idea of this symbol of warning was Jim Gray's, and took upon himself all the credit of having thus aroused the populace.

"Could Lieutenant Draper know I have been able to do so much he would be more ready to settle his account, I fancy," Hardy muttered. "If he thinks a barber's apprentice has no influence, he should look at this scene. There are nearly as many people here as saw the informer tarred and feathered, and I have had considerably more than a finger in both pies. This should show the good people of Boston what I can do. Hello, Chris! Both Christophers, eh?"

This salutation was addressed to little Chris Snyder, who was early abroad according to the agreement made on the night previous, and his companion, Christopher Gore,* a lad whom Master Snyder had brought to the scene under promise of showing him something rare.

---

* In 1809 this same Christopher Gore became Governor of the Commonwealth of Massachusetts.

" Has Master Lillie seen that yet?" Snyder asked, glee-fully, as he motioned with his thumb toward the pole.

" I can't say. I have been here only a few moments, and when I came the throng was as great as you see it now."

" It isn't reasonable to suppose the shopkeeper does n't know what has caused so great a gathering," Chris Gore said, placidly, and added, with a meaning look at Hardy, " If I had taken any part in raising that warning I should be careful to keep the fact a secret."

" Why?" Hardy asked, quickly, and looking just a trifle disturbed.

" Because more may come of it than in the case of the informer. Master Theophilus Lillie, although he may not be loved by some of us, is patronised by Governor Hutch-inson."

" Well, and what then? He made an agreement, only to break it before the words were cold, and should suffer for it," Hardy replied, defiantly.

" I am not defending him, but simply gave words to my thoughts."

" And you believe trouble will come to those who put that up?"

" I said not so, yet I believe it will be well if those who have thus advised Master Lillie keep the fact that they were concerned in the work a secret. Who is that now coming from the house?"

" Ebenezer Richardson, the informer, and Amos's uncle. Surely you should know him."

"I never saw him before, but have heard much of his doings."

"And so have others," Hardy replied, in a significant tone. "If he is wise he will stay in the house this day, for there yet remains in the city of Boston plenty of tar and feathers."

"And you think he may get a new coat?"

"It won't be long coming," the barber's apprentice replied, in a meaning tone, as if his especial mission in life was to correct the shortcomings of others. "Now that this work has been begun by the boys of Boston, it will be continued by them."

"You said that this Richardson is a relative of our friend Amos?"

"An uncle, but Amos has cast him off long since," and Hardy's assumption of importance was almost comical. "He is reading the names now; perhaps thinks he is called upon to protect Master Lillie. As I said before, he had best remain hidden from view. How Amos would rage if he could see his uncle at this moment!"

"Then he has no love for him?"

"As much as a frog has for a red rag."

The mob, who had been in the best possible humour, now began to show signs of anger as the informer made himself conspicuous, and half-muttered words soon became loudly-spoken threats.

"The informer himself should hang from that pole!"

"Where are the feathers? He needs a new coat!"

"Down with the informer!"

Richardson turned toward the mob an instant, as if to defy it, and then, as the threats grew louder, entered the house.

"Whoever did that bit of work should be well paid for it," some one in the crowd said, sufficiently loud for Hardy to hear, and the latter looked triumphantly toward Chris Snyder. "I 'll wager it came from under the Liberty Tree."

"You 're right, my friend," the barber's apprentice said, in a loud tone, and in another moment he would have revealed that which should be kept a secret, had not the arrival of several British officers given him, in his opinion, an opportunity of yet further distinguishing himself.

"There is Lieutenant Draper," he said, sufficiently loud for all in the immediate vicinity to hear, "and this time he shall listen to what I have to say, unless he is willing to settle his account."

"Are you going to speak to that officer?" Chris Gore asked, as he detained Hardy for an instant by stepping in front of him.

"Why not? He should pay that which he owes."

"But this is not the proper time to speak of business affairs. No man would listen to a barber's apprentice in public, like this."

"He shall listen to me," Master Piemont's assistant replied, loftily. "It is to me he owes the money, and I do not intend to be defrauded."

Before his companion could check him, the valiant

Hardy stepped quickly up to Lieutenant Draper, who was in company with two brother officers, and said, in an offensive tone:

"I was at the Custom House yesterday to see you, sir."

"And pray, why did you take it upon yourself to go there?" the lieutenant asked.

"Because I wanted the money you owe Master Piemont for dressing your hair, and I went where I was most likely to find you."

The lieutenant's face grew pale with anger, and he made a motion as if to strike the impudent boy, but one of his companions said, in a warning whisper:

"Be careful what you do, Draper. An injudicious word or act now might arouse this apparently peaceable assemblage into an unruly mob!"

Glancing around him, the officer realised the truth of the remark, and would have turned away but that Hardy stepped yet nearer, and, in a louder voice, cried:

"Will you give me the money now, or shall I visit the Custom House again?"

"Hark you, lad," Lieutenant Draper said, angrily, but speaking so low that only those in the immediate vicinity could hear the words, "if you dare present your barber's account to me in public, I'll have you punished for an insolent cur. When I am ready to pay your master, I will call at his shop."

"The account belongs to me. It has been turned over by Master Piemont, and the money must be paid."

" Be careful of your words, my fine fellow, or they will lead you into trouble! "

The lieutenant was now almost beside himself with anger, and, understanding that he might do something rash, his brother officers literally forced him to accompany them up the street, while the barber's apprentice, not wishing to leave the scene of what he considered his triumph, hurled insolent epithets after the soldiers.

" What are you doing, Hardy Baker? Do you want to bring about a riot? "

Turning quickly, Master Piemont's assistant saw his friend Amos, who had just come up, and he retorted :

" I am attending to my own affairs."

" It is better you should do that in private. You have no right to brawl in the streets, even though your debtor be an enemy."

" I have the right to do that which I please, and it will become you better to turn your attention to the informer, who is at the same time your relative."

" What do you mean by that? " and now Amos began to display signs of losing his temper, for the part in public affairs which Ebenezer Richardson had been playing latterly was a sore subject to him. " What has he been doing? "

" Nothing, as yet. It is what he may do that I speak of."

" But he is not here."

" He came out of Master Lillie's a few moments ago, and would have torn down the pole but for the crowd which threatened him. There he is now, and while you are watching your precious uncle, I 'll continue to demand my money from that red-coated lieutenant, if it so pleases me ! "

" Do as you choose," Amos cried, in a rage, " and some day you will realise what a fool's back deserves."

Then, understanding that no credit could be gained by bandying words with one like the barber's apprentice, he stepped nearer the two Christophers, as the mob, agitated by the sight of the informer, watched eagerly his every movement.

A wagon was coming down the street, and it appeared to Amos as if his uncle must have seen the team approaching and hurried out of the building to speak with the driver, for he made his way around the throng, as he beckoned vigourously to the newcomer.

The vehicle was a roughly-made cart for hauling country produce, drawn by two horses, and partially loaded with potatoes and corn.

The driver reined in his steeds as the informer advanced, and those nearest heard Richardson say :

" Look here, Stephen, I want you to pull your team so far in toward Master Lillie's shop that you 'll run against that pole and overturn it."

" To what purpose ? " the countryman asked, in surprise.

" It is intended as an insult to Master Lillie, and you, as one of his friends, should be willing to do so slight a favour."

" I am a friend of Theophilus Lillie in matters of business, Ebenezer Richardson ; but, when it comes to opinions, such as some of us hold and others don't, I am not favourably disposed toward the worthy merchant, as he himself well knows. What is this insult?"

The farmer descended from the wagon, and that portion of the throng which had heard his reply readily gave way before him as he advanced, until he could read the names painted on the board.

" What does it all mean?" he asked of the man standing nearest him.

" Master Lillie is one of those who agreed not to sell British goods, and has not only broken that agreement, but declares that no one shall prevent him from dealing in such wares as he thinks fit."

" But the names painted there?"

" Are those of the other merchants who believe as does Master Lillie."

" Who raised this pole?"

" That is what no one can say ; but it is safe to guess it came from under the Liberty Tree."

The farmer returned to his team, and Richardson asked, eagerly :

" Now will you run it down?"

" No, Ebenezer. It was put there by Master Lillie's townsmen, and I have no right to interfere, even though I had the inclination, which I haven't. A man who gives his word of his own free will should hold to it or take the consequences. As I said before, Master Lillie's opinions, outside of business affairs, are not my opinions."

"You are a coward!"

"I live in Massachusetts Colony, and am not willing to pay taxes for the privilege of buying goods from Britishers."

Then the farmer mounted his cart, and the crowd, wild with enthusiasm, cheered lustily his sentiments, opening a passage for him as he urged his horses forward

"You are cowards, all of you!" Richardson cried, as if beside himself with rage. "A mob of a thousand men stand by and see an old man insulted like this!"

"Your old man has laid himself open to the insult, and deserves it," some one cried.

"He shall not be forced to endure it," and the informer seized the pole as if to pull it from the ground, regarding not the shouts and threats which assailed his ears from every direction.

Now it was that Hardy Baker saw an opportunity to distinguish himself, as he thought, and, gathering a handful of pebbles from the street, he threw them viciously at Richardson.

The mob needed only an example, and, before one could have counted ten, young men and boys were pelting the informer with such missiles as came nearest to hand.

Stones, bits of earth, sticks and icicles were hurled at him with no slight accuracy of aim, and, under such a shower, the informer could do no less than beat a retreat, for to have held his ground longer would have been dangerous.

Already his face and hands were cut and bleeding, and more than once had a rock, sufficiently large to have knocked him senseless, whistled within a few inches of his head.

As he disappeared within the shop some of the younger members of the mob, chief among whom was Hardy Baker, continued to shower missiles, until they rattled against the building like hailstones; but this method of showing displeasure at the merchant's course of action was frowned down by the wiser portion of the gathering, and the boys were soon forced to desist.

"It was well enough to prevent him from taking down the pole," some one cried; "but, when it comes to destroying property, we're going beyond our rights."

"He will soon destroy that which cost so much labour to

put up!" Hardy Baker shouted. "He has only to wait until we are obliged to go away."

"That may be a longer time than he thinks for," Attucks, a mulatto who was well known to all, replied. "When it comes to such work as this we can afford to let everything else go. That pole will stand where it is a spell longer, my boy."

"But not all are of your way of thinking. It cost much labour to place it there, and it should remain until Master Lillie understands he cannot play fast and loose with the people," and now Hardy, having forced his way into the centre of the throng, was almost bursting with the desire to explain that he had assisted in this good work.

He was ready at the first opportunity to take upon himself all the credit of having devised the symbol and erected it; but there were none near who cared particularly to listen to the barber's apprentice, whose love for notoriety was his ruling passion.

Besides, even though they had been desirous of hearing what he was so eager to say, no heed would have been given his words just then, for at that moment the door of the shop was opened again, and Richardson appeared, followed by his friend, David Wilmot.

At first no one appeared to observe that the informer was armed, and then, as some one noted the fact that he carried a musket, the cry was raised :

"Down with the informer! Down with the informer! Hang him to the pole! Bring out the tar and feathers! Give him an informer's uniform!"

That portion of the mob farthest from the building, unable to see clearly what was going on, pressed forward, forcing those in front yet nearer the shop, and for an instant it appeared as if the entire assemblage was bent on making a prisoner of Richardson.

Raising his musket quickly, and, without taking aim, he fired, and as the report rang out, even above the shrill cries of the infuriated multitude, it was as if the sharp crack of the weapon had alarmed him who discharged it, for, turning precipitately, driving Wilmot before him, the informer rushed into the building, closing the door behind him.

Those in the immediate vicinity of the warning symbol, and nearest the informer, were unharmed, and, believing no injury had been done by the discharge of the musket, they set up a howl of derision, which was checked an instant later as a wailing cry came from the walk opposite.

"Chris Snyder's killed! Chris Snyder's killed!"

"Chris Gore's killed!" another cried. "Help! Stand back; you are trampling him to death!"

Turning as one man, the startled assemblage rushed frantically toward that quarter from which the ominous words had come, pressing down upon the little group that had gathered around something on the ground, until there was every danger these few would be trampled under foot.

During several moments no one outside the awe-stricken circle on the walk knew really what had occurred, and then it was whispered — not spoken — among the gathering:

" Two boys have been killed ! "

A silence that was profound, intense — a silence which was at the same time a menace, ensued, and, involuntarily, every head was bared.

Amos, who had been standing beside the two Christophers, was one of the few who knew exactly what followed the discharge of the weapon.

Little Chris Snyder, the smallest and perhaps the youngest of the throng, had fallen with an ominous-looking wound in the vicinity of his lungs, and Chris Gore was leaning against the palings, big crimson drops falling from his shoulder to the frozen earth.

Amos, at once recognising the fact that Snyder was the most grievously wounded, raised the little German lad's head tenderly on his arm as he implored those nearest to keep the crowd back, and when the excited ones in the rear finally understood what was required, every order given by Amos, boy though he was, received implicit obedience.

Rough men lifted the little lad as gently as his widowed mother could have done, and one asked :

" Where does he live ? "

" On Frog Lane.* Chris Gore must be attended to also."

" I can take care of myself. It is n't much of a hurt, this on my shoulder."

" But it ought to be dressed at once, and I am not certain you should be allowed to walk," Amos said, hurriedly.

* Now Boylston Street.

"There will be no danger; you can go with me. There are plenty who will see that poor little Chris is cared for. Some one should go ahead to tell his mother he is hurt, and to call a surgeon."

"I'll take care of that part of it," Hardy Baker cried, quickly. "Leave it to me."

Amos seized the excited barber before he could move, for he knew how Hardy would break the sad news to the poor mother, and did not intend she should suffer more than was absolutely necessary.

"Here is Master Revere!" he said, with a sigh of relief, as he struggled to prevent the apprentice from leaving him. "He is the one who should speak to Mrs. Snyder, not you, Hardy. Take hold of Chris a moment while I speak with him."

Master Piemont's assistant was not pleased at thus being prevented from appearing as one of the principal characters in this terrible drama; but Chris Gore, understanding as well as did Amos, why Hardy should not be allowed to go to the widow's home, forced him to remain by saying :

"You must stay with me until I can get home."

"Are you hurt very much?"

"It may be that I am," Gore replied, knowing that if he made light of his wounds Hardy would consider himself at liberty to act upon his own suggestion.

Hurriedly Amos explained to the goldsmith what had occurred, and what he desired the latter to do, after which he came back to his two friends.

"Master Revere will go to poor Chris's mother, and since there are more than enough to give him all the care he needs, we can attend to you."

"Do you think the little fellow will die?" Gore asked, more concerned regarding his friend than for himself.

"I am afraid the wound is a serious one," Amos replied, sadly. "The blood was coming from his mouth, and I am told that is a bad sign."

"If it's signs you're looking for, see there!" and Hardy pointed up the street, where the crowd was marching as if in procession behind those who carried the dying boy. "If that doesn't look like a funeral, what should you say it was?"

Amos gave one quick glance and turned his head away.

It seemed as if he was in a certain degree responsible for this death; but the barber's apprentice, who was equally culpable, had no such misgivings.

One would have said Hardy Baker found a certain degree of pleasure in dwelling upon the fact that he had been instrumental in this day's work, since it would bring his name into greater prominence than he could ever have hoped for otherwise, however conscientiously he might discharge his duties as Master Piemont's apprentice.

CHAPTER III.

NOT until nightfall, on this day of the tragical ending to the lesson given Master Lillie and the other faithless merchants, did Amos Richardson meet those who had aided him in the work of erecting the symbol in front of the shop on Hanover Street.

He and Hardy Baker had assisted Chris Gore to his home, and the injured boy's father had sent the barber's apprentice in search of a surgeon.

There was nothing Amos could do to aid this family, and having no desire to listen to Hardy's foolish threats, as he would probably be forced to do in case he waited for that young gentleman's return, he walked slowly toward Frog Lane, repeating again and again to himself that, if little Chris Snyder's death should follow as a result of his wound, those who had erected the symbol of warning would at least be morally responsible.

He had arrived at the Liberty Tree, where was a great throng of people waiting, as if believing that here in the so-called Liberty Hall they would the sooner receive tidings of the injured lad's condition, when he met Master Revere, returning to his place of business.

"I think, Amos," the goldsmith said, as he attracted the boy's attention by tapping him on the shoulder, "that it would be well if you were to go to the Widow Snyder's home. She may need assistance in caring for her son, and you are more to be relied upon than any lad of your age whom I know."

"Is she alone, sir?"

"Yes, so far as the interior of the dwelling is concerned; but her home is surrounded by a troop of people who think, mayhap, they show sympathy by evincing curiosity. The little dwelling was absolutely choked by those who followed Chris; but when the surgeon arrived he very rightly and promptly ordered the house to be cleared. I promised to send some person who was sufficiently clear-headed to be of service to the sorrowing widow."

"How is Chris, sir?"

"His life, probably, cannot be saved. The surgeon declares that he has but a few hours, at the most, to live; that the wound is necessarily mortal."

"Master Revere," and Amos spoke in a most sorrowful tone, "think you that those who placed the head in front of Master Lillie's shop can be blamed for the death of poor Chris?"

The goldsmith looked at Amos, searchingly, a few seconds, and then turned his eyes away.

" I think I understand why you ask that question, Amos Richardson, and sorry I am there should be the necessity for such thoughts in your mind. But he who would say those who thus attracted attention to Master Lillie's shortcomings could be held in any way as contributing to the poor boy's death, would, perforce, twist his arguments sadly. That which was done last night was not begun with any idea the ending could, by any possibility, be what it is. Therefore, while it is a most deplorable affair, one which, perhaps, may mean more than the killing of a human being, you must not let your heart be troubled. God works in wondrous ways, and who shall say that He has not shaped this for some wise purpose? Go, now, to the house of mourning, my boy, and aid that bereaved mother as best you can. Before nightfall I will send some one to relieve you of your sad duty."

Thus it was that Amos had spent the day at Frog Lane, and not until Master Revere had fulfilled his promise relative to sending another did he leave the dying lad, who was already being spoken of in the city as "the first martyr to the noble cause" and the "first victim to the cruelty and rage of oppressors."

Little Chris had not been conscious from the moment he was brought into the house, nor could any word, save that he was sinking slowly, be given to those who called at short intervals to inquire regarding his condition.

When Amos arrived at the Liberty Tree once more,

several hundred people were there, eager to learn the latest intelligence regarding Chris; but he could only make the same reply he had made so often during the day, and when it was learned that he really had no other information than this to impart, the sympathetic or the curious ones fell back, gathering in little groups to discuss the terrible events of the day, as they had been discussing them since early morning.

When he was thus left comparatively alone, Amos observed, for the first time, that Jim Gray was present at this open-air meeting; that Jim's eyes were red, as with much weeping, and that he paced to and fro, speaking to no one, even refusing to reply when accosted.

Amos understood what was in his friend's mind, and he hastened to apply the same balm with which Master Revere had cheered him.

"That's the way I have tried to figure it," Jim replied, after listening patiently to a repetition of the goldsmith's remarks on the subject. "Yet, at the same time, Amos, it is a fact that poor little Chris would not be dying this evening if we had n't taken it into our heads to give Master Lillie a warning; and whether or no it be that there is more in this than we can see now, as Master Revere proposes, we shall be forced to remember that through us, and no one else, was Chris drawn into the matter."

"But think of this, Jim: he did not receive the wound while we were putting the pole into position, but afterwards, when he was only a spectator, and he might have been there, even though knowing nothing of what was done last night."

" Yet if the pole had n't been put up he would not have been there, even as a spectator," Jim persisted.

" That is true, and I wish from the bottom of my heart that we had had no hand in it ; but it has been done now, and repentance is of no avail, so far as poor little Chris is concerned. The whole city is aroused, and I have heard those say, who should know, that most likely this will lead to the soldiers being driven out of town."

" Think you that could be done without bloodshed ? General Gage, as an officer in the King's army, has no right to leave this city unless obliged to by force of arms."

" Whatever may come of it, I know not ; but — "

" Well, I can tell you," and Hardy Baker, who had approached unobserved, stepped in front of his two friends with the air of one whose shoulders are weighted heavily with burden of state. " Of course I am in a way to hear a good deal more than you fellows because so many of Master Piemont's patrons are Britishers. The ' bloody backs ' themselves say this is really the beginning of insubordination in the Colonies, and before many months have passed the King will find it necessary to punish us severely. It may be learned that we won't submit as readily as they seem to fancy."

" But how could it be avoided ? " Amos asked, impatiently ; for the tone in which the barber's apprentice spoke, and the swagger he had assumed, grated harshly upon the boy's nerves.

"We'll arouse the people to action," Hardy replied, loftily.

"Yes, and in the meanwhile the King will have sent over more soldiers to whip us into submission. If such men as Master Adams are unable to remedy this state of affairs, I don't believe the yoke of oppression, which bears so heavily upon the Colonies, will be removed by any effort at Master Piemont's hair-dressing shop."

"It is all very well for you to sneer when you don't understand the situation; but your harsh words won't alter the facts, and I tell you, Amos Richardson, you will see yet more blood spilled."

"And you propose to take a hand in the spilling, I suppose?"

"I shall be wherever anything of the kind is going on, of that you may rest assured. Do you know where your uncle is at this moment?"

"No."

"The people made prisoners of Wilmot and him, and carried them both to Faneuil Hall, where they have been examined and committed for trial. He will be hanged for murder."

"As he should be, even though he is my uncle! But when that has been done, what then?"

"You shall see," the barber's apprentice replied, in a prophetic tone. "I am not through with this matter yet."

Then Master Baker walked slowly away, as if the fate of the Colony of Massachusetts was in his keeping.

The interview with Master Piemont's assistant did not serve to cheer either Amos or Jim, but rather further distressed them in mind, and, after trying in vain each to give some comfort to the other, the two went to Chris Gore's home, where they learned that he was resting comfortably, in no danger of death.

On the following morning the tolling of the bell on New Brick Church told that little Chris Snyder was dead, and the city was in more of a ferment, if possible, than before.

Liberty Hall was crowded with people who had gathered to discuss the situation of affairs, which now seemed dangerous in the extreme, and threats against the " bloody backs " were openly indulged in.

Amos and Jim were together the greater portion of the time which intervened between Chris's death and his funeral ; but saw nothing of the barber's apprentice.

They had been selected, together with four others of the dead boy's friends, to act as pall-bearers, and on Monday forenoon performed their part in the impressive ceremonies, which were held under the Liberty Tree, when beneath it was placed for a brief time the coffin bearing on its head the inscription, *"Innocentia nusquam tuta ;"* on the foot, *"Latat anguis in herba ;"* and on either side, *"Hæret lateri lethalis arundo."*

Four hundred schoolboys marched in couples behind the casket containing all that was mortal of Chris Snyder ; thirteen hundred citizens followed, and the procession was closed by thirty chariots and chaises.

The bells of Boston and the neighbouring towns were tolled as the procession marched from Frog Lane to the Liberty Tree, and from thence to the burying-ground, and on every hand the little fellow was spoken of as the "first martyr in the cause of American liberty."

During the week which followed the funeral ceremonies, Amos and Jim were much together in the home of Chris Gore, whose wound was rapidly healing. They had little or no intercourse with the barber's apprentice, whom, it was rumoured, had made friends among a certain set of men frequenting the resorts on the water-front of the city.

Neither had succeeded in convincing himself he was wholly blameless for the tragedy on Hanover Street, and both shunned Hardy Baker as much as possible because of the ridiculous threats he made as to what he intended to do, and cause others to do, against the soldiers.

It was on the Friday succeeding the funeral, when Amos and Jim were together in the yard of the latter's home, where the symbol of warning to Master Lillie had been prepared, that the barber's apprentice burst in upon them like a whirlwind.

Excitement was written on every feature of his face, and several seconds elapsed before he could speak coherently. Then he exclaimed:

"It has come at last! It has come at last!"

"What has come?" Amos asked, impatiently.

"The 'bloody backs' are to be driven out of town. They have done so much this time that the people will soon put an end to them! It seems that Chris Snyder's murder was n't enough — "

"But the soldiers had nothing to do with that," Jim said, quickly. "We three are the guilty ones."

"Now you are talking foolishly," Hardy cried, angrily. "If I did n't know you two fellows as well as I do, I 'd say you were ready to make friends with the oppressors."

"We have no desire to be friendly with the soldiers," Amos replied, thoughtfully, "nor can I understand why we should announce ourselves as their enemies. They have done nothing to us personally; but are simply stationed here in obedience to the King's commands."

"Oh, they have done nothing to us, eh?" the barber's apprentice cried, as if in a fury. "You stand here and say that, after what has happened this afternoon?"

"Well, what *has* happened?" and Jim caught the excited barber by the coat collar, shaking him vigorously, as if he believed by such energetic measures he might be restored to his scanty senses.

"Come down under the Liberty Tree and you 'll find out all about it. I tell you that this sort of thing can't go on much longer. We 'll rise in our might, as Attucks says; that 's what we 'll do, and I 'll help in the rising!"

"Instead of continuing such ridiculous threats as you have been making since the funeral, suppose you tell us what happened this afternoon to put you in such a state of excitement. Has some other Britisher refused to pay your master's bill?"

"This is a matter which the people of Boston must take

up, and that's exactly what they will do?" Hardy cried,
stammering in his eagerness to relate the exciting news.
"This forenoon one of the 'bloody backs' was down by
your father's ropewalk,* and got into a little trouble with
one of the workmen. Nothing would do but that they
must fight it out, and the redcoat got a beating."

"Well?" Amos asked, placidly, as Hardy paused for
breath.

"Well, and what does the Britisher do, but walk straight
up to Murray's Barracks,† get a crowd of his chums, and
go back to Gray's place, where they pounded five or six
of the rope-makers almost to death. While you fellows
have been sitting here idle, people who have more love for
their country are gathering under the Liberty Tree, and if
you go there now you'll hear what is to be done."

Jim looked at Amos as if to ask whether he believed
all the barber's apprentice had told them, and the latter
replied by an incredulous shake of the head, as he said:

"We'll go down to Liberty Hall; but I don't think the
inhabitants of Boston are nearly as much excited as Hardy
believes. He and that mulatto friend of his, I reckon, are
the only ones representing the people in this case."

"Come with me, and you will soon see who is doing the
representing," Hardy cried, angrily. "You fellows don't
know everything, even though you think you do."

"We have never made claim to such distinction, nor do

---

* John Gray's ropewalk was situated near the present Post Office
Square.

† Near the former site of Brattle Street Church.

we believe we are expected to drive the redcoats out of
Boston. But if the city is in such a turmoil as you would
have us think, why are you here, instead of at Liberty
Hall?"

"I have been there since an hour before noon, and only
left when I had to go for something to eat. Now I am on
my way back."

"We'll go with you," and Amos began to believe that
perhaps there was more truth in Hardy's story than he
had previously been willing to admit. "Have you aban-
doned Master Piemont entirely?" he asked, as the three
went into the street.

"I may go back there when the Britishers are driven
away; but it ain't likely I shall much before then. When
there's work like this to be done, you'll find me with those
who love their country."

"And that is brawling on the waterside, I suppose?"

Hardy was about to make an angry reply, when a throng
of men and boys were seen marching in something approaching military precision up Corn Hill, shouting from
time to time :

"Drive the rascals out! Down with the 'bloody
backs!'"

Now there could no longer be any question in the minds
of Jim and Amos but that Hardy's story was more nearly
true than was at first believed, and immediately they began
to share his excitement.

"Perhaps you think now that I'm the only one who is
stirred up, eh?" the barber's apprentice asked, trium-

phantly. "This crowd is going to Liberty Hall. When you get there you 'll find more than a thousand, all shouting the same thing."

That which caused Amos and Jim more surprise than anything else, was the fact that not a soldier could be seen upon the streets. Ordinarily one could not walk through Corn Hill without meeting many privates, as well as officers, lounging on the sidewalk.

That the citizens were deeply excited over what had occurred, both the boys understood as they continued on toward the common meeting-place; but they had no idea how deeply the populace were moved, until arriving within sight of the Liberty Tree, where they saw the ground immediately beneath its broad limbs literally packed with human beings.

The gathering in front of Master Theophilus Lillie's shop had been as nothing compared with this.

There the throng had been composed chiefly of boys, but here men were gathered, and Amos had a better idea of the gravity of the situation when he recognised on the outskirts of the crowd reputable merchants, whom he knew could not be easily induced to lend countenance to anything which did not really affect the welfare of the Colony.

Forcing their way here and there among the excited multitude, where were a dozen speakers, each haranguing those nearest him, the boys learned that the determination of the citizens was that the soldiers should be forced to leave the city, and that the affray between the military and the rope-makers was but an incident which had

brought about the uprising at this particular time, rather than something to be avenged.

They also heard that the mob had assembled near the barracks early in the afternoon for the evident purpose of taking up the quarrel of the workmen, but had been dispersed by the troops.

It was also reported that the commanding officer of the Twenty-ninth Regiment had made formal complaint to Lieutenant-Governor Hutchinson, not only of the insults which his men had received at the rope-walk, but from the citizens at different times.

" They take possession of the city against our expressed will, and now complain because they are not treated politely!" one of the speakers cried. " Their ideas of gentle breeding are so different from ours that the only amends we can make for our rudeness is to give them an emphatic invitation to go elsewhere in search of people who love redcoats."

"Down with the 'bloody backs'! Drive them out! They have no business here!" the crowd shouted, and for a moment Amos and Jim believed a desperate conflict was near at hand.

The more violent of the speakers were followed by merchants who deprecated any hasty movement, and in a short time that which had been almost an ungovernable mob was rapidly becoming an assemblage of earnest, thinking citizens, desirous of doing in a crisis that which would best and most effectually right the wrongs under which they were suffering.

"This is a work which cannot be done in a day," a venerable looking gentleman said, when some on the outskirts of the crowd demanded to be led to the barracks. "What is begun now must be finished. To make the demand that the British soldiers leave the city, and not enforce it, would be far worse than to remain silent. Much time may be needed."

"We have all there is. No other work shall be done until this job is finished!" one of the company cried.

"Then set about it methodically," the orator continued. "To-day is Friday, and in an hour it will be ended. If we begin on Saturday, we may be tempted to desecrate the Sabbath; therefore, as good citizens, I pray that you will first consider your duty to your God, and not forget to keep holy His day. The soldiers will be here on Monday. Let us begin our work then, and finish it before the following Saturday night."

There was something in this suggestion which pleased the throng wonderfully well. The idea of remaining inactive forty-eight hours rather than take the chances of desecrating the Sabbath pleased them, because it savoured of more serious purpose than if they had begun hurriedly, without preparation, like an unreasoning mob, to open the struggle.

There were a few, however, who raised their voices against this delay, and Amos whispered to Jim, as a particularly shrill cry was heard now and then demanding that something be done immediately:

"That is Hardy Baker! He believes that he has brought

all this about, and if it should be that the soldiers are
driven from the city, he will claim the whole credit."

"This will be more serious than warning Master Lillie,
terrible as was the result there. What shall we do, Amos?"

"Follow these gentlemen, of course," and Amos
pointed to several well-known citizens, who were standing near by. "We cannot do anything wrong by acting
with them; but I question much if the morrow will pass
without serious brawls, for Hardy Baker and those with
whom he is associated are ripe for mischief, regardless of
the justice of their cause."

"But can we, unarmed, drive the soldiers out of the city?"

"When such a man as Master Samuel Adams declares
they must go, and is backed by these good citizens here,
Governor Hutchinson and General Gage must listen to
the voice of the people. Come over this way; Hardy
and Attucks are moving toward us, and I don't care to
be seen in their company."

Amos had not observed the barber's apprentice soon
enough to escape him, for, before he and Jim had taken a
dozen steps toward hiding themselves among the throng,
Hardy Baker shouted, shrilly:

"Hold on, boys! We want to talk with you!"

Jim would have continued on, regardless of the command, but that his companion said, in a whisper:

"We may as well wait and hear what he has to say,
otherwise he will follow wherever we go."

"I want you fellows to come with Attucks and me,"
the barber's apprentice said, in a peremptory tone.

"Why should we?" Amos asked, sharply.

"Because there is work for all hands, and you must do your share."

"And since when has Master Piemont's apprentice had the right to command us to come here or go there?"

"Your high and mighty airs don't count for much with me, Amos Richardson. If my uncle had been the one who murdered Chris Snyder, I should try to do everything in my power to show I didn't side with informers and those who are ready to kiss the feet of the 'bloody backs'!"

Amos's face was almost livid in its paleness, as he stepped quickly forward and seized by the collar the apprentice, who, in his alarm, attempted to seek refuge behind the mulatto.

"If you ever so much as mention my uncle to me again, Hardy Baker, there will be serious trouble for you, and neither the 'bloody backs' nor those who love liberty will interfere between us."

Then Amos, shaking Master Piemont's assistant much as a terrier shakes a rat, released his hold, and, as he walked away with his arm in Jim's, he heard Hardy cry, threateningly:

"Before this trouble is ended, you shall see what I can do!"

"It is such fellows as he who will bring discredit on the cause of liberty," Jim whispered. "You must be careful from this out, Amos, or that braggart will make good his threat."

CHAPTER IV.

A DISCOMFITED CREDITOR.

ON Saturday morning the city of Boston was in an
ominous state of quietude.

That the citizens were restless and uneasy, even the
most casual observer would have noted, as he walked
through the streets where knots of men and boys were
congregated at different points, discussing some subject
with bated breath, and moving away whenever a stranger
approached.

That the troops were defiant and suspicious was also
evident. The soldiers did not walk through the streets
singly, as had been their custom; but in groups — squads
would be a more appropriate term, for they preserved
some semblance of formation, even while lounging, as if
prepared for an expected attack.

It had not been Amos's purpose to venture out on this
morning, and he had very good reasons for remaining at
home.

That which Hardy Baker had taunted him with on the
evening previous still rankled in his mind, and he understood better now than before the encounter at Liberty
Hall, that there were many who would not hesitate to
remind him of the fact that it was his uncle who had de-

prived little Chris Snyder of life — his uncle, the informer, who had been the first to resist, with deadly weapons, the citizens in a demand for justice.

Amos was not a quarrelsome lad ; although the acknowledged leader in his particular circle of friends, he had never been a bully, neither had he submitted tamely to an imposition.

He was fully determined to give Hardy Baker such a lesson on the evils of using his tongue ill-advisedly and without precaution, as he would not soon forget, although he did not intend to seek an interview with the apprentice, who fancied himself rapidly becoming a leader of men ; but proposed to wait until he met the barber by chance rather than intention, and then he was resolved that Hardy should receive a very clear idea as to the necessity of curbing his speech.

The forenoon was well advanced when Jim Gray entered the house with an exclamation of surprise and satisfaction.

" I never counted on finding you at home on this day of all others ; but just dropped in on the chance you might be here, since I have looked everywhere else.   Why are you keeping so snug when there is so much going on ? "

" What is being done ?   I heard no noise, and thought everything was quiet."

" It is not what is being done, as what may happen at any time,'' Jim replied, thoughtfully.   " There is mischief in the air, and Liberty Hall is packed as full as it was last night."

" Surely the people will do nothing to-day, for it was

understood yesterday that no demonstration was to be made until Monday."

" According to my way of thinking only a word is necessary to bring about considerable trouble. It is said that the citizens have demanded the removal of the troops, but Master Hutchinson will not listen to their complaints."

" And if he does not, how can anything be effected? Surely the people of Boston will not try conclusions against a regiment of soldiers."

" Some of the crowd are in the humour for anything desperate, and they are the ones with whom Hardy Baker has made friends. He is talking very fiercely now, and showing his blackened eye freely as a reason why there should be no delay in forcing the soldiers to leave the city."

" A blackened eye? Has he been fighting already?"

" I don't think he had much chance to do anything of that sort ; but this is the story he told Chris Gore, from whose home I have just come: After the meeting last night, and when it had been fully decided that nothing should be done until Monday, Hardy, having an idea the Britishers would be frightened, thought it a good time to demand payment from Lieutenant Draper. Without heeding the warning which the officer gave him on the morning poor little Chris Snyder was killed, Hardy went to the Custom House again this forenoon, and says he simply asked to see the lieutenant ; but most likely he was as insulting as when he met that officer on Hanover Street. The sentry knocked him down, and now Hardy shows the, wound as his claim to be considered a living martyr. It

may be exactly as he says, that the soldier had no provocation, other than the demand to see the lieutenant; but
I don't believe that portion of the story, for after yesterday's troubles it is n't reasonable to suppose the troops
would invite another conflict with the citizens.   It is said
they have been ordered to hold no communication whatever with the people, and it is positive that the sentry at
the Custom House struck Hardy."

"I suppose he is now more violent than ever?"

"Yes, and has a stronger belief that his countrymen
depend upon him to avenge their wrongs.   Come down to
Liberty Hall, and see him make a spectacle of himself."

"I think it is wiser for me to stay here."

"Why?" Jim asked, in surprise.

"Because, if I should meet Hardy now, while he is so
puffed up with pride because he has been attacked by one
of the enemy, he might say something which would lead
to an encounter between us; and I don't think it would
be well to raise any disturbance on the street at this
time."

"Perhaps you are right; but yet—"

Jim was interrupted by the noise as of a heavy blow
against the side of the house, which was repeated half a
dozen times before either of the boys could step to the
window.

Then came threatening cries:

"We have got one Richardson in jail; now bring out
the others!"

"Drive out the informers!"

" Boston is no place for assassins ! "

By this time Amos and Jim were where they could look into the street ; but a view of what was taking place there was not necessary to explain to them the cause of this sudden attack.

They knew that Master Piemont's assistant was making good his threat of the previous evening.

Ten or a dozen half-grown boys, with the barber's apprentice at their head, were pelting the house with missiles of every kind, and Amos's mother cried frantically, as her son was on the point of rushing out to put an end to the disturbance :

" Don't show yourself, my boy, don't show yourself ! After what has happened, we must expect that the sins of your uncle will in some degree be visited upon us, and you must do nothing rash, particularly while your father is away from home."

" But, mother, this is only some of Hardy Baker's doings, and I can soon put an end to it, once I get that precious little villain by the throat."

" You would add to the disgrace by fighting on the street ? "

" I would show the barber's apprentice that he can't insult honest people without bearing the consequences."

" Come on ! " Jim cried, impatiently. " Two of us can handle that crowd ! "

Mrs. Richardson clung to her son imploringly, crying that he would be killed if he ventured into the street, and there seemed good reason for her fears, since if any one of the missiles, which were being hurled so freely against the building, should strike him, it would inflict serious injury.

As the moments passed and no reply was made by the inmates of the house to the epithets, Harry's squad grew bolder. Instead of contenting themselves with defacing the building, they proceeded to do all the damage possible.

The more serious mischief was begun by the barber's apprentice himself, as he threw a lump of frozen earth directly through the window, causing the splintered glass to fly in every direction, and one of the fragments struck Mrs. Richardson on the cheek with sufficient force to draw blood.

Amos could no longer control his temper; shaking off his mother's detaining grasp, he flung open the outer door, and, followed closely by Jim, leaped directly into the midst of the throng.

More than one of the missiles struck him; but he was not conscious of the fact. He only saw Hardy Baker, and had no other thought than that by administering swift punishment to him the attack would be brought to an end.

Master Piemont's assistant saw his late friends making

their way directly toward him, regardless of every one else, and understood their purpose.

It had not been his intention to have a personal encounter with Amos.

He had recruited his squad from the more turbulent and violent spirits gathered under the Liberty Tree, and believed it was sufficiently large to protect him. Being their leader, he supposed every member of the party would be on the alert to defend him ; but in this he was mistaken.

As soon as Amos and Jim showed themselves, the shower of missiles ceased, and the mischief - makers stepped aside to give them free passage.

" Close up here ! " Hardy shouted, frantically. " Why are you fellows backing down now ? There are enough of us to flog the life out of this portion of the murderer's family ! Stand by me ! Are you going to allow both these boys to do as they please, without your lifting a hand ? "

" Only one of us will deal with you, Hardy Baker," Amos cried angrily, as he seized him by the collar. " Stand back, Jim, and see that I have fair play. There's no need of your doing anything, unless this barber's gang do as he asks them."

" Help ! Help ! Come here, some of you fellows ! What did you promise before we left Liberty Hall ? " Hardy shouted frantically, as he writhed in Amos's clutch.

One or two of the party made a movement, as if they

would answer this appeal; but Jim Gray, although he had no appearance of an athlete, looked particularly dangerous as he said, sharply:

"If you are wise, you'll keep your distance. Hardy Baker brought you here to insult honest people who would scorn to have dealings with informers, even though they do chance to be of the same family. He lied to you, and you should let him attend to his own affairs. It is an even-handed battle, and both shall have fair play so far as I am concerned."

"That is all any fellow could ask for," one of the party cried, forgetting, in his desire to witness the encounter, that he had come on an alleged public mission. "If you'll agree not to touch our man, we will see to it that yours has his rights."

"That's all I want," Jim replied, grimly, and added to Amos, who, still holding Hardy firmly by the collar, had stopped to learn what part the barber's followers proposed to take: "Now is your time; the rest of these fellows agree to fair play, and I reckon no one will disturb you."

Hardy Baker was terrified, as could be told by the expression on his face, and he cried, shrilly:

"Why don't some of you cowards do as you agreed, and stand by me?"

"That's what we're going to do," the boy who had spoken with Jim replied. "No one shall interfere, and you said it wouldn't take you five minutes to disable Amos Richardson for life. Now go ahead and do it. If any one attempts to help him, we'll pitch in."

There was no further opportunity for the barber's apprentice to appeal to his followers.

Shaking him vigorously, as if with the idea that after such treatment he could better understand the words, Amos said, in a tone sufficiently loud for all to hear :

" I came out here simply to give you a flogging, Hardy Baker, and did not intend to waste any time about it ; but so long as your friends are willing to stand by honestly, you shall have a chance to prove you can do what you boasted of being able to do."

Then Amos released his hold of the barber's collar, in order that the latter might be in a position to defend himself.

Hardy could do no less than strike out in his own defence, for it was not possible to beat a retreat ; but his efforts were as feeble as they were vain. Before five minutes had passed Master Piemont's assistant was the most thoroughly whipped boy in the Colony of Massachusetts, and perfectly willing to acknowledge himself such, if by so doing he could prevent a continuation of the punishment.

" I can't strike a fellow when he will no longer defend himself," Amos said, as if in apology, after Hardy was so cowed as to remain passive under the blows. " I don't reckon you other fellows really knew what you were about when you came here to raise a row, so we 'll let the matter end here. Until last night this barber and I were good friends, and would have been this moment, but for the fact that I refused to make a street brawler of myself, as he demanded. It is true Ebenezer Richardson is my uncle ; but neither my father nor myself are of his way of thinking, as this whipped cur knows thoroughly well.   I have been as ready to cry down an informer as any of you, therefore why should my father's house be attacked ? "

"He told us you were hand in glove with the ' bloody backs,' " one of the party said, as he motioned toward the prostrate barber.

"And he was lying. Ask any of the boys who know me whether that is true. You can believe Chris Gore, who was wounded the same day Chris Snyder was killed ; ask him ! "

"And why not ask me?" Jim Gray cried.   "It was Amos Richardson who had charge of putting the warning in front of Master Lillie's store."

"Hardy Baker said he and Chris Snyder did that alone," one of the barber's followers shouted, and Jim replied :

"All the part he took was to help carry the pole from my house over to Hanover Street. Amos had charge of the whole matter, and yet you believe he is friendly with the ' bloody backs,' just because he happens to have an uncle who is no honour to the family."

"We should n't have known anything about it, but for the barber, and if you think he has n't had enough, we 'll finish flogging him."

Hardy, who had not dared to move from the moment Amos ceased punishing him, now looked even more terrified than before, until the latter replied :

"No good will come of abusing him. Let him alone, and in the future I reckon he 'll tell the truth."

"He will never tell us anything again that we shall believe," one of the attacking party said. "I'm sorry we let a liar like him lead us on to what we've done against you, and I'll agree we won't make such a mistake again, if you'll call it settled. Come down to the Liberty Tree with us, you two fellows, and let's see what's going on there."

Amos, eager to get the throng away from his father's house, accepted the invitation at once, and he and Jim marched in the midst of their late enemies, while Master Piemont's assistant was left alone to nurse, at the same time, his wounds and his anger.

The throng at Liberty Hall was as great as Amos had ever seen it at any time; but decidedly more quiet and orderly than on the previous evening.

It was as if, having decided upon a definite plan, the people were willing to wait quietly until the hour set for action should arrive.

It was rumoured that the Sons of Liberty, as an organisation, had agreed to head the populace in a peremptory demand for the removal of the troops, which was to be made on the following Monday; but Amos failed to learn that there was any good foundation for this rumour. It was known positively that the Sons of Liberty had laid the grievances of the people before the Governor and Council, but there were many at Liberty Hall who doubted if the members of the Society would countenance the actions of the mob.

"It seems as if poor little Chris was forgotten already,"

Jim Gray said, after he and Amos had listened to several hot-headed speakers urging the people to rise in their might. "Now they talk only of the attack upon the rope-makers, and hardly mention his name."

"That is because the trouble at your father's ropewalk was brought about by the soldiers, while Chris was murdered by one of our own people, if we are willing to acknowledge that Ebenezer Richardson was one of us."

"Does he never visit at your house?"

"He hasn't since the day Master John Hancock was arrested in regard to the seizure of his sloop. That was the first time he showed himself an enemy to the Colonies, and father declared he was no longer a brother of his. Don't talk about him any longer. It's a subject that makes me sick at heart. Suppose we go down to see Chris Gore? It will be better than standing here listening to these men, who have but little idea of the subject they are pretending to discuss.

The wound on Chris's shoulder was healing rapidly; but it was not deemed safe for him to venture out-of-doors yet, and his comrades felt it their duty to give him a detailed account of all that had occurred during the day.

The snow was beginning to fall when Amos and Jim left Mr. Gore's home, and before the next morning it had covered the earth with a mantle of dazzling whiteness.

CHAPTER V.

A NIGHT OF TERROR.

AMOS and Jim were early astir on Monday morning, the fifth of March, but before noon came both were convinced that the threatened trouble would blow over without the slightest semblance of a conflict between the soldiers and the citizens.

During the forenoon they had not so much as heard of Hardy Baker, or that faction to which he had allied himself, and Jim said, with a quiet chuckle of satisfaction:

"I reckon the barber got as much of a lesson as he needed Saturday afternoon, and has given over trying to set right the wrongs of the people."

"He must be at work, or we should have heard something regarding him," Amos replied, and then ceased even to think of the apprentice.

Shortly after noon those assembled under the Liberty Tree, — and there were quite as many as had gathered on Friday and Saturday, — were told that the Council had discussed with Governor Hutchinson the question of removing the troops from the city, and assured him the people would be satisfied with nothing else.

It was also said the Governor had refused to do anything regarding the matter; but that Samuel Adams had publicly declared the troops should be sent away, and that without loss of time.

At about three o'clock in the afternoon, Amos and Jim heard once more from Master Piemont's assistant.

It was told under the Liberty Tree that he had been seen in company with Attucks, the mulatto, and half a dozen others, near Wentworth's Wharf, and that Hardy had distinguished himself by taunting with cowardice, a squad of soldiers, until the redcoats avenged the insults with blows; but nothing more serious than a street brawl was the result.

"Perhaps I made a mistake, and Hardy did n't get as severe a lesson as he needed," Jim whispered to his friend.

"If he did n't, he's likely to receive it before this day is ended, in case he continues as they claim he has begun. It seems evident that the citizens do not intend to carry this matter any further, and the only trouble may be from such as Hardy. Let us go home and stay there quietly. If the Sons of Liberty were to make any demonstration, we would want to be with them; but if there is to be nothing more than street brawls, we had better keep out of sight."

Jim was perfectly willing to act upon this suggestion, and particularly because his father had warned him not to go in the vicinity of the ropewalk, fearing lest the trouble, having originated there, it would be a favourite rendezvous for those ripe for mischief.

The boys had hardly reached Amos's home, thoroughly

confident there would be no serious disturbance, when the alarm-bells began to ring, and, as in the twinkling of an eye, the city, which had apparently been so peaceful, was the scene of tumult and confusion.

Men and boys rushed from their homes into the streets. Those who were already there ran to and fro in the wildest excitement, not understanding the cause of the alarm, and prudent housewives barred windows and doors as if each thought her home was about to be attacked.

As a matter of course, Amos and Jim went directly to the Liberty Tree; but failed to find there the throng which had occupied Liberty Hall almost constantly, with the exception of the Sabbath hours, since Friday morning.

" The soldiers have attacked the citizens ! " a man cried, as he ran up Newbury Street at full speed.

"Where? Where?" Amos shouted.

" At the head of King Street."

The few who were waiting at Liberty Hall started immediately for the scene of the supposed conflict, and Amos and Jim followed their example.

The boys had no idea of mingling in street brawls ; but if unoffending citizens were attacked by the soldiers, it was their intention to aid the former to the best of their abilities.

Before they could traverse the distance between Essex and King Streets, the alarm-bells had ceased ringing, and they met a throng of citizens returning from the supposed scene of violence with information that no outrage had been committed.

Samuel Gray, Jim's elder brother, was standing at the corner of Summer and Marlborough Streets when the two boys arrived at that point, and he explained the cause of the commotion by saying:

" A party of citizens, not over-gentle in their ways, attempted to pass the sentinel near the barracks, and were received by him at the point of his bayonet. One of our people was scratched slightly on the arm, and at the sight of the blood some one more timid than wise alarmed the city. You can go back, boys, for your services are not needed. Take my advice, Jim, and keep off the streets."

" But I intend to be on hand if there is any serious trouble."

" I should hope so, for you are old enough, if not large enough, to do your full share. What I meant was, don't get mixed up in street fights between the soldiers and disreputable citizens whose proper place is in the watch-house."

" I don't count on doing anything of that kind. Where are you going?"

" Up to Liberty Hall."

Amos and Jim followed, and, arriving at this common rendezvous, they found that the people were once more assembled; but this time in not as placid a humour as before.

The news of the encounter, and the needless alarm, had so excited the people that the more impetuous ones were in such a frame of mind that prudence would not be their first counsellor.

The city, which had been in an apparent state of quietude an hour previous, was now in a tumult, and when a
squad of eight soldiers marched past the Liberty Tree, as
if defying the people, they were received with epithets of
derision and a shower of missiles thrown by the angry
members of the party.

The cooler-headed men and boys did their best to
restrain their companions, and the result was that the
soldiers passed on, after indulging in a few threats.

" One can see how easily a fight may be brought about
just now," Samuel Gray said to Amos. " The people are
ripe for almost any kind of trouble, and if the authorities
were wise the soldiers would not be allowed to show themselves on the streets."

" It seems as if those fellows passed this way simply to
provoke us."

" Very likely they did; but it is n't because of such
provocation that we should resort to bloodshed. Our part
is to preserve the peace, if possible, while men like Master
Samuel Adams redress our wrongs in a proper fashion. I
doubt not but that through his influence the soldiers will
be forced to leave the city; but nothing of the kind can
be brought about by street brawls and foolish threats.

The excitement among those gathered at Liberty Hall,
— and there were now very many reputable citizens present, — was most intense, and continued to increase each
instant.

Word was brought of collisions between soldiers and
citizens at different points, and although very much of the

information was afterwards ascertained to be untrue, no one questioned it at the moment.

It seemed apparent to all that the time had arrived when the question as to whether the soldiery should be allowed to occupy Boston must be settled by force of arms, despite the odds which must necessarily be against the inhabitants in such an encounter.

Before sunset on this day the situation seemed to have changed greatly, for the brawlers of Hardy Baker's class were now in the minority, and it was sober, well-meaning citizens who occupied the space under the Liberty Tree.

Rumours came thick and fast. Some claimed that the Sons of Liberty, as an association, had that afternoon demanded of Governor Hutchinson that the troops be withdrawn; others declared the demand had been made and positively rejected, while the more timid insisted that the soldiers were making ready to awe the citizens by such a display of power, regardless as to whether bloodshed might ensue, and that within the next twenty-four hours there would be found no one bold enough to demand that they be sent away.

Amos and Jim, believing themselves in good company so long as they remained with Samuel Gray, kept close at his heels, and he was not loth to have them, for, like many another in the city of Boston on this night, he was firmly convinced that the strength of boys, as well as men, would be necessary before morning to preserve the slight semblance of freedom which was left to the Colonies.

John Gray's fears that there would be trouble in the

vicinity of the rope-walk had been proven by this time to be groundless, for soldiers as well as citizens had, as if by common impulse, avoided the scene of the first serious outbreak, and at seven o'clock in the evening, when the city was more nearly in a state of repose than it had been since the alarm-bells sum- moned the inhabitants, Samuel Gray proposed to his brother and Amos that they go to the fac- tory.

"I promised father I would look around there now and then, and if you boys are not counting on going home to supper, I can give you something in the way of a lunch from the store of provisions I carried there this morning."

"We are certainly not going home while there seems to be so much afoot," Amos replied.

"Then come with me, and we'll hope that the intentions of those who are abroad this night are as peaceable as ours."

It was destined, however, that they should not partake of the provisions which Jim's brother had stored for such an occasion as this.

On arriving at John Gray's place of business, a party numbering twenty or thirty, led by Attucks, with Master Piemont's assistant by his side, was seen marching toward the Custom House, shouting and hooting, as if to prove their courage by much noise.

"It is by such as them that mischief may be done," Amos said, in a low tone. "Hardy Baker cares not what statements he makes, so long as he appears to be considered a leader," and he concluded by telling Sam the story of the attack made the previous Saturday afternoon.

"I grant you the barber's apprentice is a dangerous sort of a lad to be loose at a time like this. Nevertheless, there are reputable citizens who believe the moment has come when we should stand for our rights, and what such as Hardy Baker may succeed in bringing about, through their folly, will perchance aid the righteous cause. We will follow them."

"To what purpose?"

"In order to learn if there is any preconcerted action among them. It was whispered at Liberty Hall late this afternoon that arrangements had been made for a demonstration in front of the barracks, and I would be there if such is made."

"But do you believe in anything of that kind?" Amos asked, in surprise.

"Certainly I do, my lad. If Governor Hutchinson insists it is not the desire of reputable citizens that the soldiers be sent away, it seems necessary he should be convinced of his mistake, and —"

"Surely Hardy Baker and Attucks, and their following, would not be taken for reputable citizens?"

"True, lad, but at the same time they echo the sentiments of even such men as Master Samuel Adams. Do you observe that in all this excitement no one in authority among us has advised that we remain quiet ? It appears to me they are willing matters should take their course, and will not attempt to prevent the hotheads, hoping that through unreasoning violence good shall come."

Amos, remembering all he had heard since the murder of little Chris, began to believe Jim's brother was correct in his statement. He knew full well that if Master Samuel Adams or Master John Hancock requested the citizens to desist from gathering on the street, or from making any demonstration against the soldiers, their wishes would have been respected, and such brawlers as Hardy Baker been forced to remain quiet.

It was a revelation to him that a noble purpose might be attained through ignoble means, and immediately he ceased to regard the barber's apprentice as a menace to the public peace.

The party, headed by Attucks, continued straight on toward Dock Square, and at nearly the same time a like party came down from King Street, while yet another could be seen at the head of Union Street.

No less than six hundred men were now approaching a common centre with cries of :

" Let us drive out these rascals ! They have no business here ! Drive them out !"

" It is as was rumoured," Sam Gray said, quietly. " There is concerted action here, and before morning Governor Hutchinson will understand that it is the citizens of Boston, not a rabble, who demand the removal of the troops. If the better class of people wish the red-

coats to remain, why do not some of them stand here to
prevent mischief?"

Jim made no reply. He already realised that this was
a movement of the populace, and not an ordinary street
brawl.

Each moment the crowd that had assembled in the
square increased in numbers; but it remained as orderly
a gathering as ever assembled at Liberty Hall until a
squad of soldiers, evidently for no other purpose than to
show their contempt of the people, strode into the square,
forcing a passage through the crowd in an offensive and
insolent manner.

Then came that cry which aroused those who heard it
more quickly than had the pealing of the alarm-bell.

"Town-born, turn out! Down with the 'bloody backs'!"

The soldiers lost their air of security and defiance as
these words were passed from one side of the square to the
other like the waves of the sea, and caught up in every
direction by those on the adjacent streets, until it seemed
as if the very air was tremulous with the cry:

"Town-born, turn out!"

The soldiers disappeared; but the summons for those
who would defend their city's rights had so excited even
the cooler-headed ones that action was an absolute necessity, and yet no leader had at that moment arisen to map
out a course of action.

If their movements were concerted up to the time of
meeting in Dock Square, it was evident the plan of oper-
ations had not been carried further than that, and the

excited ones looked about eagerly for the enemy, but, seeing none, began to vent their fury on inanimate objects.

The market stalls were torn down that the timbers might be used as weapons ; the fire-bells rang out their brazen peals ; here and there men excited almost to the verge of frenzy discharged a musket or pistol in the air, and constantly were the numbers of the throng increased, until Amos and Jim thought it was as if all the male inhabitants of the city had gathered in one place to defend the town.

The pealing of the bells brought to the tumultuous scene those who did not sympathise with the movement, as well as those that approved of it, and among the former class were several well-known citizens, who, believing the greatest danger was to be apprehended from such an uprising, endeavoured, by all their powers of persuasion, to induce the people to return to their homes, leaving to such as Adams and Hancock the task of ridding the city of the redcoats.

So earnestly did these peacemakers labour that the respectful attention of the greater portion of the gathering was soon secured, and even those who brandished weapons, calling frantically to their comrades to follow them to the barracks, listened, half persuaded, to the words of these temperate men.

In half an hour the shouting, yelling throng had so far been reduced to silence that Amos believed all danger of violence was over, when suddenly there sprang up, as

if from the very ground beneath them, a tall man dressed
in a scarlet cloak, his head covered with a white, flowing
wig, and, mounting the wreck of the market stalls, he
stood, a commanding figure, illumined by the rays of the
moon.

"You have come here as men determined to obtain
your rights," he cried, in a ringing voice, which could be
heard distinctly by all, "and will you depart as children?
Will you listen to those who counsel soft words when you
are confronted by the muskets of your enemies? Will
you, town-born, be thrust aside by the Britishers at every
corner of the streets? Have you come here simply to
shriek for your rights, and then to disperse quietly, lest
you displease the hirelings of the King? Are you afraid
of punishment which may follow, that you would slink
away now? It is the town-born who must defend the
town. It is the town-born who shall relieve the town from
the burden under which it groans, and it is the town-born
who this night should appear before the main guard as
their masters, not as their servants."

"To the main guard! To the main guard!"

The multitude caught up the cry, and as if in a twinkling the throng was in motion, each pressing forward by
the nearest way toward the barracks.

The streets were choked with people, and as the vast
throng spread itself out toward the nearest approach to
the quarters of the guard, they were, by force of circumstances, divided into three divisions.

Samuel Gray and his two companions were carried,

without effort on their part, with one of these bodies, and, by a singular chance, pressed into close companionship with the barber's apprentice and his comrades.

The direction taken by this last division led them directly past the Custom House, and as they approached it Amos heard the shrill voice of Hardy, high above the cries and shouts of his companions :

" There 's the scoundrel who knocked me down ! That sentinel in the doorway blackened my eye because I dared ask to see Lieutenant Draper ! "

The attention of the throng was thus directed to the single soldier who stood on duty at the Custom House.

" Knock him down as well ! Give him a dose of his own medicine ! "

" Death to the ' bloody backs ' ! "

" Kill him ! Kill him ! "

Now the excited ones no longer thought of the main guard. They saw before them an armed enemy, and he it was who had abused one of the town-born.

Some continued to utter threats ; but many flung bits of ice, frozen dirt, and even such harmless missiles as snow-balls, while not a few pressed toward the soldier, as if to make him prisoner.

The man looked down upon his assailants defiantly, and, as if to show more clearly what punishment it was possible for him to inflict upon them, began deliberately to load his musket.

This action intensified the anger of the younger people, and they pressed yet closer.

"Advance one step further, and I kill the man nearest!" the sentinel cried.

"If you fire you must die for it!" Henry Knox * shouted from among the throng.

"I shall shoot if they come nearer!"

As he said this the soldier levelled his weapon, evidently determined to execute the threat, and at the same time he shouted lustily for the main guard.

"That's right! Bring on your main guard! But we'll kill you first," Attucks cried, fiercely, as he made a dash forward, forcing his way through the press, owing to his great strength.

Before he could reach the sentinel, Captain Preston, the officer of the day, with a guard of eight men, came on the double quick from the Town House, and forced his way, at the point of the bayonet, to the sentinel's side. Once there, the newcomers provoked the throng to yet greater fury, as they repeated the action of the sentinel, by loading their muskets deliberately.

There were but few among that gathering who were not carried away by the excitement of the moment; yet some retained their presence of mind, and among these last was Henry Knox, who, calling several nearest him to his assistance, succeeded in gaining Captain Preston's side.

There, seizing the officer's arm, to attract his attention, he cried, imploringly:

"For God's sake, take your men back, Captain! Your life and theirs will pay the penalty of an encounter now!

* Afterwards Washington's Secretary of War.

The mob are beside themselves with rage, and this small squad could do nothing against them, once they were let loose."

The officer shook off his well-meaning adviser as he ordered his men to stand firm and defend themselves with their bayonets.

How it happened Amos never really understood; it was as if, while he was yet calm and collected, a sudden flare had come across his eyes, and he realised nothing more until he was in the foremost of the throng, pressing eagerly forward toward the red-coated enemy, without regard to possible danger, as he joined those around him in yelling and hooting.

Men and boys in the rear were firing whatever missiles came to hand, and friends were struck as often as foes.

Amos heard some one cry, and he thought it was Attucks:

"Let us fall upon the guards! The main guard! The main guard!"

He saw, as if in a dream, the mulatto beat down the musket of a soldier with a club; he heard those directly behind him cheering wildly, and he added his voice to theirs.

Somewhere from the rear came the cries:

"Don't be afraid of them!"

"They dare n't fire!"

"Kill them! Kill them!"

He half turned his head, believing it was Jim who had raised the last cry, and just at that instant he saw the

mulatto aim a blow at Captain Preston's head with the
club; he understood that it was parried by the officer's
arms, and then noted with satisfaction the fact that as the
weapon descended it knocked a musket from the hands
of a soldier.

It was to him more like a dream than a reality when
he saw the mulatto raise the musket quickly, as if to use
it upon the officer, and at that moment some one, Amos
never knew who, shouted:

"Why don't you fire? Why don't you fire?"

Instantly, above the shouts and yells of the multitude,
was heard the sharp, ominous crack of a musket, then
another and another, until six reports seemed literally to
cleave the air, while before him, and on either side of
him, Amos saw men fall; saw the crimson blood gushing
from gaping wounds, and then it was as if consciousness
deserted him.

CHAPTER VI.

AFTER THE MASSACRE.

A MOS was brought to a consciousness of his surroundings by the wailings of Jim, who, regardless of everything save his own sore affliction, was kneeling by the side of his brother, trying to staunch a sluggish flow of blood, which was issuing from Sam's forehead.

Near him lay James Caldwell and Crispus Attucks, both of whom had been killed instantly, and a short distance away Samuel Maverick and Patrick Carr were writhing in the agony of mortal wounds, while here and there within the narrow space were six others who had been brought to the ground by the leaden hail.

Amos dimly understood that the crowd had fallen back at the discharge of the weapons, but he thought only of his friend's great grief, and tried in vain to assuage it.

Sitting upon the snow-covered ice, Jim held the head of his dead brother, moaning and sobbing, until Amos began to fear he also had been wounded.

"Did any of the bullets hit you, Jim?" he asked, solicitously.

"No, no, I only wish they had! *I* don't amount to anything. Poor Sam!" And, in the frenzy of his grief,

Jim swayed to and fro, still holding in tender clasp the lifeless head, while above him, grim and menacing, stood the soldiers with levelled muskets.

While one might have counted twenty, the square, lately the scene of such an uproar, was silent, save for the moans of the wounded, and then the tramp of the soldiers rang out horribly distinct as Captain Preston marched them away to the main guard.

The people recovered sufficiently from their terror and bewilderment to advance, in order to succour those who were suffering, and hardly had they done so when the sound of drums beating the call to arms was heard, and a few moments later it was whispered from one to another that the Twenty-ninth Regiment was forming in ranks near the Town House.

Then from far up the street came the dreadful cry, shrill and menacing:

"The soldiers are rising! To arms! To arms! Turn out with your guns!"

While the drums continued to beat, this terrible summons resounded through first one street and then another, striking terror to the hearts of those who heard it; but causing the courageous to hasten to the scene of the murder in order to aid their townsmen, and the cowardly to seek refuge in flight.

Five minutes later, amid the rattle of drums and the menacing cries, came the pealing of bells summoning the inhabitants to defend their city.

In Dock Square men stood shoulder to shoulder, the well-to-do citizen by the side of the labourer or sailor, each armed after his own fashion, and each ready to defend the lives of those nearest and dearest to him.

During half an hour or more there was probably no person in the vicinity of the tragedy who did not firmly believe that the soldiers were rising with the intent to massacre, and then Governor Hutchinson appeared upon the scene, ordering the people to disperse, and declaring the "law should have its course."

"Has the captain who ordered the soldiers to fire been arrested?" some one cried, and instantly there went up a great shout.

"Arrest the murderers! Bring them to justice before you call upon us to go quietly to our homes! Murder has been done this night, and the blood must be avenged!"

The Governor hesitated, as if uncertain what reply should be made, and then said:

"Justice shall be meted out to all. You who have gathered here have done so in defiance of the law, and — "

"We have come here that the law shall not be broken,"

a voice cried. "Arrest those who have committed the murder! Do your own duty before you call upon us to do ours."

The Governor attempted once more to speak, but the cries of the more ignorant ones drowned his voice, and he disappeared from view.

Shortly after, while the citizens remained in an attitude of defiance, it was reported that Governor Hutchinson had ordered Captain Preston to be brought before him, and that an investigation of the officer's conduct would be made.

Then a portion of the people returned to their homes; but yet more remained to make certain the report regarding the investigation was not a falsehood, devised for the purpose of inducing them to disperse.

Of all these things Amos knew nothing. His thoughts were confined entirely to his grief-stricken friend, and as he assisted in carrying Sam to his brother's house on Royal Exchange Lane, he moved and acted like one in a dream, for the terror of the scene was still upon him.

He left Jim by the side of the lifeless body, while kindly friends hastened to break the sad news with some degree of gentleness to the parents of the murdered man, and then went to his own home; but not to sleep.

It was not yet daylight, on the following morning, when Christopher Gore, his arm bandaged and in a sling, appeared at Amos's home.

" I was afraid you might have come to some harm when I heard that Sam Gray was killed, for I knew you and Jim were most likely near him," he said, as if apologising for his early visit. "How did you escape?"

"I don't know, Chris. It does n't seem to me that I can remember anything of that awful moment, except that I saw Sam Gray fall dead, and heard Jim weeping over him."

"Do you know what became of Hardy Baker?"

"I did n't see him after the shots were fired. I only know it was he who called attention to the sentinel, and but for him it is almost certain no disturbance would have taken place at the Custom House. Have you heard from him?"

"No. I wanted to go out as soon as we heard that murder had been done; but mother would n't listen to me. It was only by promising to come directly here, and have you walk home with me, that she was willing I should venture out now. The streets are filled with people, and the excitement is as great as at noonday."

"Have you heard whether the British captain has been arrested?"

"Father said, and he was among those who waited to be certain Governor Hutchinson would n't play us false, that the investigation was not finished until three o'clock this morning. The captain has been held for trial, and the squad of soldiers who did the firing are all in jail."

"Do you know what is to be done now?"

"There is to be a town meeting at Faneuil Hall at eleven o'clock, and it is said that Master Samuel Adams will address the people."

"Are you to be there?"

"I would n't dare go in a crowd while the wound on my arm is yet unhealed. What have you to do this morning?"

"Why do you ask?"

"I wanted you to come to my home with me; but I suppose that is too much to ask, for of course you intend to be on the street, in order to know what is going on."

"I 'll go with you willingly, Chris. I have seen enough of the work which may be done on the street, until the time comes when I can be of some assistance."

An hour later the boys were at Chris Gore's home, and there they remained until noon, when it was learned that a formal town meeting was appointed for three o'clock in the afternoon. During the informal meeting Master Samuel Adams had made an address to the people, in which he recommended that a committee be sent to the Governor, to tell him once more that peace could not be maintained while the British soldiers virtually held possession of the city, and of this committee was Master Samuel Adams.

At night, when Chris Gore's father came home, he reported all the general public knew regarding the condition of affairs.

Faneuil Hall had proven too small for the throng of citizens assembled at the hour set, and it became necessary to adjourn to the Old South Meeting-house.

There it was said by some one who claimed to have talked with one of the committee appointed to wait upon

the Governor, that while the throng were passing from
Faneuil Hall to the church a member of the Council said
to Hutchinson :

" This multitude are not such as pulled down your
house ; but they are men of the best character, men of
estates, men of religion, and men who pray over what they
do."

" When Master Adams came into the meeting-house at

the head of the committee," Mr. Gore said to the boys, in
continuing his story, " he whispered to those who were
nearest as he passed, and I was one of them, ' Both regiments or none ! Both regiments or none ! ' I did not at
the moment understand his meaning ; but a few moments
later, when the report had been read, all was clear. Lieutenant-Governor Hutchinson had decided that both regiments could not be removed ; one must remain. The
Twenty-ninth, because it was members of that body who
committed the murder, was to be sent to the Castle ; but

the Fourteenth, so the Lieutenant-Governor declared, was
to remain in the city.   Then we knew what Master Adams
meant by his whispered communication, and the cry went
up in such volume as seemed to shake the building, ' Both
regiments or none.'

"With this as the sentiment of the people, little business was done, save that of making plain to Governor
Hutchinson that our will, not his, must prevail.   A new
committee, of which were Master Samuel Adams, John
Hancock, and Dr. Joseph Warren, was chosen, and sent
to the Council-chamber to report.   I was so fortunate as
to be able to speak with Dr. Warren shortly after they
returned, and am, therefore, able to tell you exactly what
occurred.   Master Adams, in presenting the case for the
second time to Governor Hutchinson, argued as he always
has, that it is illegal to quarter troops upon the city in
time of peace, and that this, if there was no other reason,
would be sufficient cause for our demanding their immediate removal.   The Lieutenant-Governor insisted it
was not only legal, but absolutely necessary, and he lamely
concluded by saying the soldiers were not under his control.   Then it was Master Adams took advantage of this
weak point in His Excellency's remarks, to say that if he
had the power to remove one, he could remove both regiments, and he added — I can well fancy with what power
— 'A multitude, highly incensed, now awaits the result
of this application.   The voice of ten thousand freemen
demands that both regiments be forthwith removed.
Their voice must be respected — their demand obeyed.

Fail not, then, at your peril, to comply with this request. On you alone rests the responsibility of this decision ; but if the just expectations of the people are disappointed, you must be answerable to God and your country for the fatal consequences that must ensue.' "

" And then he could do no less than comply with the demands of the people," Chris said, excitedly.

" He did nothing of the kind, my son ; but declared that he would not allow himself to be intimidated ; that he should not send both regiments away. What the result might have been had the committee returned with this decision, I tremble to contemplate ; but Lieutenant-Colonel Dalrymple, who, it seems, has a better idea of the condition of affairs in this city than the men who rule over us, gave his word of honour as a soldier that the troops should be removed at once, and such was the report with which the committee returned to us."

" And does the matter rest there, sir ? " Amos asked.

" Yes, to a certain extent. The people, determined there should be no opportunity of breaking faith, either on the part of the Lieutenant-Governor or the military officer, appointed the same gentlemen who had waited on His Excellency, as a Committee of Safety, and from this time out our most reputable citizens will act as night-watch, each doing his share of the duty fully armed, until every soldier shall have left this city. There is to be no unnecessary delay."

" But what about those who committed the murder ? "

" They will be tried in due form, and I hope, as must

every good citizen, that it will be an impartial trial.
Already it is claimed for Captain Preston that he did not
give the order for his men to fire; but that some one
near him — perhaps one of our own people — seeing the
soldiers were threatened with bodily harm, and that there
was every danger of their receiving severe injuries, cried:
'Why don't you fire?'"

"And that is exactly what I heard," Amos said,
quickly. "I was looking at the captain at that fatal
moment, and, although it had n't occurred to me from
that time until this, I am certain he never gave the command to fire. Nevertheless, the soldiers all shot to kill."

"True, lad," Mr. Gore said, sorrowfully, "and if the
military remain in the city, it will be impossible for the
authorities to prevent further conflicts, more especially
now that the people are fully aroused by the bloodshed."

When Amos set out for home at a late hour that evening, he saw the members of the citizens' watch parading
the streets, and there came to him a sense of deepest
relief after the terrible events of the past week, with the
knowledge that for a certain time, at least, the good city
of Boston would be properly guarded by her own people.

Despite this new feeling of safety, he started with
apprehension, almost alarm, when a dark figure crept
cautiously toward him as he was passing the head of
Water Street, and an instant later he stood with his
back against the palings in an attitude of self-defence,
for he who had approached so stealthily was Hardy Baker.

"Don't act as if you was going to fight me," the

barber's apprentice said, piteously. " Don't do that, Amos! I know I tried to make trouble for you yesterday afternoon ; but you served me out for it, and I have n't said a word against you since then."

" I don't know whether you have or not."

" What I tell you is true, Amos," and the listener was thoroughly surprised by the change in the bearing of Master Piemont's apprentice.

" What do you want of me ? " he asked, sharply.

" I don't know," Hardy replied, in a tone of despair. " It seems as if everybody was my enemy. I went down to Jim Gray's house this afternoon, and he would n't so much as look at me."

" Do you think he has good reason to be friendly with you ? "

" You say that because his brother was killed at the Custom House. Amos, I did n't think anything like murder could happen when I told the crowd the soldier on the steps was the one who had knocked me down. If you had been treated as I was, and saw the man standing there when you believed the soldiers were going to rise against us, you might have done the same thing."

" Well, and if I might, what then, Hardy Baker ? What do you want of me ? "

" I want you to talk with me, Amos. It seems as if everybody believed I was as much of a murderer as the ' bloody backs,' and Master Piemont told me this afternoon never to show my face near his shop again — that I was n't wholesome even for Britishers to look at."

"I don't think, Hardy," and now Amos's tone was less sharp than before, "that you should expect either the people or the soldiers would be very friendly toward you."

"But I didn't do this thing. I didn't have any more hand in it than you, or Jim Gray, or Chris Snyder."

"But how can you charge us with any concern in it?"

"Was n't it all a piece of work beginning with what we did to Master Lillie? Has n't it grown out of that?"

"Of course not. Ebenezer Richardson's bloody deed had nothing to do with the soldiers," Amos cried, quickly, but at the same time a terrible fear took possession of him that possibly the tragedy on Hanover Street might have had some connection with that at the Custom House.

"But, Amos," Hardy continued, imploringly, "when poor little Chris Snyder was killed through what we did to Master Lillie, and you were as much concerned in the matter as I, you did n't accuse me then of being at fault."

"No," Amos said, slowly and thoughtfully, "because that which we did, so Master Revere said, was not done with any idea or possibility in our minds that bloodshed might follow."

"Nor was there in my mind any idea that bloodshed might follow when I told the crowd the soldier at the Custom House was the one who had knocked me down."

During several moments Amos stood silent and motionless.

Hardy's offending seemed less heinous in his eyes than it had a few moments previous, and he said, in a milder tone;

"I won't be one to accuse you, Hardy; but let me advise you to leave the affairs of the city to those who are older and have better judgment. Don't go about any more with such companions as have been yours during the past few days."

"Will you forgive me, Amos, for what I did yesterday?"

"I surely ought to, after we settled it with our fists."

"May I walk home with you?" Hardy asked, meekly, after a brief pause.

"To what end?"

"I want to be with some one who is friendly," and Master Piemont's assistant spoke in a tone of such dejection that Amos's heart was touched.

"Where do you live?"

"Nowhere now. Master Piemont declares I shall not stay in the house another hour — you know the terms of my apprenticeship were that he should give me a home."

"Then what do you intend to do, Hardy?" and now Amos began to display some concern.

"I shall walk to Salem, where my parents live, if I cannot find other work here. I am afraid when people know it was through me that the trouble began at the Custom House, they will feel as Master Piemont does, and refuse to hire me."

"You can't walk to Salem to-night. Where will you sleep?"

"That makes no difference. If you will only be friendly with me, Amos, I can get along somehow."

"You shall go home with me, Hardy, and after the excitement has died away people will begin to realise that you are not as much to blame as now appears. Even Jim Gray will see the matter in another light, as soon as his grief has subsided."

With this reconciliation it is necessary, because the purpose of this book is finished, to bid adieu to the boys whom we have met under the Liberty Tree, for in nowise would the incidents of their lives interest the reader, until after the lapse of many months, when we may, perchance, meet them again, while relating certain events connected with the Siege of Boston.

The following is taken from Arthur Gilman's "Story of Boston."

"Before the troops could be removed, on the following Thursday, March 8th, the funerals of the slain were celebrated with all the pomp that Boston was capable of displaying at the time. The assemblage was the 'largest ever known'; the bells were tolled in Boston, Cambridge, Roxbury, Charlestown; the bodies of Caldwell and Attucks, the friendless ones among the victims, were taken to Faneuil Hall, Maverick's was borne from his mother's home, on Union Street, and that of Gray from his brother's on Royal Exchange Lane. The four hearses formed a junction on the fatal King Street, and thence the procession continued, six deep, to the Middle, or Granary Burying-ground, where the bodies were solemnly laid in a single grave. Thus, the last view that the retreating soldiers had of King Street was marked by the passage of thousands of Bostonians, doing honour to the men whose taunts and insults had goaded them beyond endurance, and they felt the humiliation of their situation as they gave way before the successful 'bullies' of the little town, who had put them to flight. It was not 'ignominious' in Dalrymple, however, to take his men away from an infuriated populace; there were then thousands of sturdy New Englanders in the towns about, ready to crowd into Boston at the proper signal; and what were two single regiments to do if they had come? It was foolhardy in Hutchinson to resist the demand of the determined gathering at the Old South. He had been wise the evening before, but on that day his sagacity deserted him. When Lord North, the unwise minister of King George, heard of the circumstances, he was interested in every detail, and the picture of Adams before Hutchinson impressed him so deeply that he afterwards called the Fourteenth and the Twenty-ninth 'the Sam Adams regiments.'"

"In August, 1775, the name of Liberty having become offensive to the tories and their British allies, the tree was cut down by a party led by one Job Williams. 'Armed with axes they made a furious attack upon it. After a long spell of laughing and grinning, sweating, swearing, and foaming, with malice diabolical, they cut down the tree, because it bore the name of Liberty.' (Essex Gazette, 1775.) Some idea of the size of the tree may be formed from the fact that it made fourteen cords of wood. The jesting at the expense of the Sons of Liberty had a sorry conclusion; one of the soldiers, in attempting to remove a limb, fell to the pavement and was killed."

—Drake's " Old Landmarks of Boston."

THE END.